Chapter 1
The funnest of fun!

It was the same every Saturday.

The very *best* sort of same.

Because Saturday was the day that Zac and his cousin, Essie, got to visit Granny Mo – all by themselves! Almost.

Granny Mo lived a short bus trip away.

And so this Saturday, the same as always, Zac's mum walked him to the bus stop round the corner from their flat. And, the same as always, Essie's dad walked her round the corner from their house. Along came the bus and the two cousins got on it together.

"Bye, Mum! Bye, Uncle Matt!" said Zac.

"Bye, Dad! Bye, Auntie Tara!" said Essie.

After they had said goodbye, Zac and Essie said hello to the bus driver. And then they argued for the rest of the short trip to visit Granny Mo.

First they argued about who got to sit next to the window.

"It's *my* turn!" said Zac.

"No, *you* sat beside the window last time!" Essie grumbled.

Then they argued about who was going to press the button to stop the bus.

Contents

"It's *my* turn!" said Essie.

"No, it's *my* turn!" said Zac. He put out his arm and ding-ding went the button before his cousin could press it first.

The bus slowed down outside a row of shops. The door opened with a SWOOSH.

There was Granny Mo. She waited for them by the bus stop every single Saturday.

"Well, hello, my little monsters!" she said in her happy sing-song way.

"Hi, Granny Mo!" said Zac and Essie. They jumped off the bus with matching big smiles.

Zac and Essie loved their granny from the top of her head to the tips of her toes. They loved her ruby-red hair, they loved her stripy socks, they loved everything about her. She made everything sunny. She made grumbles pop like bubbles.

"What are we going to do today, Granny Mo?" asked Zac.

Granny Mo lived in a flat above the shops. She put her key in the lock of the bright red door that led up to her flat.

"Wait and see!" she said with a wink at Essie and Zac.

Zac and Essie grinned at each other as they ran up the stairs.

Things were always fun with Granny Mo. The funnest of fun!

Last week they'd had a picnic at the park and *all* the food was purple. The week before it had rained and Granny Mo had built an obstacle course in the hallway. It was made out of teetering towers of boxes, wobbly piles of cushions and perfect pyramids of loo roll.

So what was Granny Mo's plan today?

Hmm ...

Maybe it had something to do with the scritchy-scratchy noise coming from the other side of the door to Granny's flat?

Chapter 2
Granny Mo's surprise

As soon as Granny Mo opened the door, a small shadow shot off into the living room.

"Me first!" said Essie as she rushed after it.

"No, *me* first!" said Zac as he tried to get in before Essie.

"Slow down, you two!" Granny Mo called out. "You'll scare her!"

"Scare who?" asked Essie.

She and Zac looked around the empty room and saw nothing and no one.

Then they heard a tiny sound from behind the sofa.

"Meep!"

"What was that?" asked Zac.

"Granny Mo – have you got a cat?" Essie asked.

"Not exactly ..." said Granny Mo. She got down on her hands and knees and made "ppzzz-whzzzz" noises.

A soft brown nose popped out from behind the sofa.

"Well, it *looks* like a cat to me!" said Essie, getting on her hands and knees too.

"And me!" said Zac as he stood and looked down at the twitchy nose and whiskers.

"I've decided to get a pet," said Granny Mo. "But I can't decide what sort of pet to get. So my friends are going to lend me *their* pets, to see what suits me best. I haven't got a cat; I've borrowed one. This is Wilma's cat, Cookie."

As she spoke, a shy cat slipped all the way out from behind the sofa and rubbed herself against Granny Mo's face.

"Awww!" said Zac and Essie.

"Meep!" said Cookie the cat.

"Foof!" said Granny Mo. She rubbed a tickly cat hair away from her nose.

"So will you help me look after Cookie today, and a different pet every Saturday for the next few weeks?" Granny Mo asked Zac and Essie.

Essie felt a flutter in her tummy. She was excited. Her dad was allergic to animals, so Essie didn't have a pet of her own. And Zac's block of flats had a big, cross "NO PETS!" sign in the hall.

"YES!!!" Zac and Essie shouted *very* loudly.

"MEOWWWW!" The shy cat jumped. Cookie didn't like loud noises.

She jumped up onto Essie's head.

"OOH!" Essie yelped.

Then Cookie jumped down and ran right up Zac's leg as if he were a tree.

"OW!!" he called out.

When the cat got to Zac's neck, she jumped onto the curtain.

RIP! Cookie's sharp claws tore the curtain.

Next she jumped onto the shelf over the fireplace and – CLUNK-CLINK-PLINK! – all Granny Mo's nice things crashed onto the floor.

ZOOM, ZOOM, ZOOM! went the cat. She whizzed around the flat six times in a row till they all felt dizzy.

"OH NO!" yelled Essie when she saw the cat slither out of the door that led to the roof terrace.

Granny Mo ran and grabbed Cookie *just* before she jumped after a pigeon flying by.

*

Cookie's owner collected her at teatime. Granny Mo, Zac and Essie sat slumped on the sofa. They were tired after chasing Cookie about all day.

"You know something?" said Granny Mo. "I think cats are too *zoomy*. Perhaps I'd like a *different* sort of pet."

Essie smoothed her hair where Cookie had messed it up. Zac rubbed his leg where Cookie had climbed up.

Maybe a different pet *would* be more fun. Maybe one with not so many claws ...

Chapter 3
The perfect pet?

Over the next few Saturdays, Granny Mo borrowed a lot of pets.

After Cookie the zoomy cat, there was a yellow spotted snake called Samson.

"Isn't he beautiful? He's a corn snake," said Granny Mo.

If Samson was stretched out, he'd be as long as Granny's arm. But now he was twirled around her wrist like a chunky bracelet!

"Can I hold him?" asked Zac.

"Can I hold Samson *first*?" asked Essie.

Granny Mo smiled at them both.

"I think a snake is *exactly* the sort of pet I need!" she said.

But almost as soon as she said it, Samson slid off Granny Mo's arm and vanished down the back of the sofa. He didn't come out for the rest of the morning.

"You know something?" said Granny Mo. "I think snakes might be too *tricky* to look after. Maybe I should think of *another* pet."

*

After Samson the snake, Granny Mo borrowed a bunny called Rocky.

"He's a house rabbit!" said Granny Mo. "Look, he has a tray of food and a tray of hay to use as a toilet."

Rocky's fur was as soft as a cloud. Essie stroked him first, but Zac was first to feed him a carrot. After that Rocky hop-hop-hopped around the flat, sniffing and snuffling at everything.

"I think a house rabbit is *exactly* the sort of pet I need!" said Granny Mo.

But an hour later she changed her mind. Rocky hadn't just sniffled and snuffled at everything in the flat. He'd nibbled on it too.

"You know something?" said Granny Mo as she held up the chewed TV cable. "I think house rabbits might be too *nibbly*. Maybe I should try another kind of pet."

*

After Rocky the house rabbit, Granny Mo borrowed a squawky chicken called Chickpea.

"A chicken could live on my terrace," said Granny Mo. "And it'll give me eggs!"

Zac and Essie liked the little wooden house that Chickpea's owner left for her. They liked the way Chickpea walked, with her head bob-bob-bobbing.

They had a contest to see who could bob-bob-bob most like Chickpea. Granny Mo was the judge and said they were *both* winners.

"I think a chicken is *exactly* the sort of pet I need!" said Granny Mo.

But then Chickpea pecked *all* the petals off *all* the flowers in *all* the pots and left them all over the floor. After that, Granny Mo wasn't so keen.

"You know something?" she said. "I think chickens might be too *messy*. Perhaps a more relaxed pet would suit me better."

*

After Chickpea the chicken, Granny Mo borrowed a ... well, Zac and Essie had no idea what it was.

The pet that Granny had borrowed floated in a tank of water on the table. It was pale pink with a red ruff around its neck. It had four legs, a tail and tiny black eyes.

"Is it a sort of fish?" asked Zac.

"Don't be silly!" Essie said to him. "What kind of fish has *legs?*"

It looked more like a cross between a frog and a tiny lizard.

"Its name is Arlo and it's an axolotl from Mexico," said Granny Mo.

She noticed that both her grandchildren looked puzzled.

"It *is* a tricky name to say. Think of it like this: AXE – OH – LOT – ILL!"

Zac and Essie tried saying "axolotl" a few times.

"I think an axolotl is *exactly* the sort of pet I need!" said Granny Mo.

But later that day she changed her mind. The axolotl floated for hours in the tank and didn't move at all. It just stared and stared and *stared* at Granny Mo and Zac and Essie.

"You know something?" said Granny Mo.

What Granny Mo said next took Zac and Essie by surprise …

"Animals take a lot of looking after," said Granny Mo. "Maybe I'm not meant to have a pet."

"Aw!" said Zac and Essie at the same time.

"No, it's all right," Granny Mo said with a smile. "After all, I *do* have you two little monsters to keep me company every Saturday!"

Her bright sunshine-y smile made Zac and Essie feel better.

"And when you come next week, how about I think of something super fun for us to do?" said Granny Mo.

Zac and Essie both nodded.

They were sorry Granny Mo had changed her mind about getting a pet. But they loved being her two little monsters – for ever and ever and always!

Chapter 4
Follow me ...

The next Saturday rolled around.

The bus door opened with a SWOOSH!

Zac and Essie were ready for the super-fun thing Granny Mo had planned.

"Well, hello, my little monsters!" Granny Mo called out to them, just like normal.

The two cousins jumped off the bus and went to give their granny a hug.

But something got in the way of the hugging.
Granny Mo had a big bright canvas bag across
her chest. It was stuffed full. And she had a
plastic bucket and spade in each hand.

"Here!" said Granny Mo. She gave the red
bucket and spade to Essie, and the green bucket
and spade to Zac.

"Are we going to the beach?" asked Zac. The
beach was far away and Zac didn't have his
swim shorts.

"Nope," said Granny Mo as she set off along
the street. She made a jingle-jangle noise with
every step because of the pretty silver bells
sewn on to her bright canvas bag.

"Where *are* we going then?" asked Essie as
she jogged along to keep up.

"You'll soon see!" said Granny Mo with a
grin.

*

With some turning this way and turning that way and no clues at *all*, at last they came to a low wall that ran along by the river.

"Right!" said Granny Mo. "Follow me ..."

She walked down ten stone steps that led to
the river, with Zac and Essie close behind.

But not a lot of the river was there today.
Only a ribbon of water ran down the middle,
with gloopy-looking sand banks on both sides.

Zac and Essie knew that meant it was "low tide". They'd learned about tides in school. Low tide was when the sea slurped the water away, before it rolled right back in later for high tide.

"So, are we ready to go mudlarking?" asked Granny Mo as the three of them stood together on the bottom step.

Zac and Essie looked at each other and frowned. What did Granny Mo mean?

"Sorry, I couldn't hear you," joked Granny Mo, and put her hand to her ear. "I said, ARE WE READY FOR MUDLARKING?!"

"Er, what exactly *is* mudlarking?" asked Essie.

"The sand banks are *full* of stuff that people have dropped over the years," Granny Mo told them. "And mudlarking means you dig in the muddy sand to see what you can find. Like a treasure hunt!"

"YESSSS!" yelled Zac and Essie with two high fives and a clatter of buckets.

Treasure hunting sounded very good fun indeed!

Chapter 5
Thing in the mud!

"Let's get started," said Granny Mo. "Take off your shoes and roll up your trousers."

The cousins put down their buckets and spades and did as they were told.

Zac slipped off his trainers and put them on the stone step next to each other. Then he rolled his joggers up above his pink knees.

Essie kicked off her sandals and threw them down next to Zac's shoes. She scrunched her leggings up past her brown knees.

The bells on Granny Mo's bag jingle-jangled as she bent down and untied her rainbow laces. As soon as she set her own shoes next to Zac and Essie's, she walked off onto the gloopy wet sand. Her feet sank into it.

"It looks more like cold porridge than sand at the beach," muttered Zac.

Essie thought so too. She pushed her big toe into the wet, sandy ooze and she didn't know if she liked it much.

With a shlurp and a plop, Granny Mo pulled her feet out of the sucky sand and turned round to look back at Essie and Zac.

"Come on, you two!" Granny Mo called out.

The cousins were still standing on the bottom stone step. For once they didn't argue about who was going first. They didn't want to go *anywhere* till they found out more.

"What sort of treasure will we find?"
asked Essie.

"Maybe some old bottles or buttons!" said
Granny Mo with a WOW sort of smile.

Zac and Essie looked at each other. That didn't sound too WOW to them.

"Or maybe some old Roman money if we're lucky!" Granny Mo said. "So hurry up and let's get digging."

Granny Mo pulled a small garden spade out of her big jingle-jangle bag.

But the two cousins *still* didn't move off the last stone step. They were frowning at something that was right beside their gran ...

"Granny Mo, what is *that?*" said Essie.

"What is what?" said Granny Mo.

She turned round and saw a small mound of mud that was getting slowly bigger and bigger right next to where she was standing.

Bigger and bigger, like a fat bubble in a pot of soup, just about to pop.

Only *this* brown bubble got bigger and bigger and *bigger*, till it was as high as Granny Mo's knobbly knees.

And it *didn't* go pop.

It stayed exactly where it was ... and blinked two round googly eyes at them all!

Chapter 6
The odd blob

Granny Mo had said they might find treasure in the sand banks.

Old buttons or bottles or Roman money maybe.

She didn't say anything about a googly eyed mud mound!

"Aahhh!" Zac yelled.

"What *is* it?" squeaked Essie.

"Some sort of animal, of course!" said
Granny Mo, and bent down to look at it. "You're
an odd-looking thing, aren't you?" she said.

It *did* look odd. A bit like a balloon dipped
in melted chocolate. Just a big blob of mud with
eyes. The mud was so thick it was hard to tell if
the blob had skin or fur, or how many arms or
legs it had. Two? Six?

Zac and Essie forgot to be scared and started to think about what it could be.

"Is it a dog?" asked Essie. She stepped onto the sand bank to have a look and she forgot about the ooze squishing between her toes.

"Or an octopus?" said Zac, and stepped into the mud too.

"I'm not sure," said Granny Mo.

She was looking right at the thing.

The googly eyes blinked back up at her.

Granny Mo held out her hand – the thing sniffed it.

"Is it hurt?" asked Zac. "Do we need to take it to a vet?"

"Or lost?" asked Essie. "Do we need to find its owner?"

"Let's take it home and clean it up," said Granny Mo. "Once we see what it is, we can work out what to do next."

Granny Mo put her hand inside her jingle-jangle bag and pulled out a stripy beach towel.

"I *was* going to use this for drying our feet after mudlarking," said Granny Mo. "I didn't think I'd need it for an animal rescue!"

Granny Mo put the towel around the thing and gently lifted it up.

It didn't wriggle or squiggle.

It just blinked its googly eyes at her.

"Can *I* carry it?" asked Zac.

"Can I carry it *first*?" asked Essie.

But even if the cousins were arguing again, they still smiled at each other.

Saturdays were *always* fun with Granny Mo. But today was the best fun ever – and super exciting too!

Chapter 7
Tiny treasures

When they got back to Granny's flat, she put the thing in the bath. Then she washed the muddy sand off with lots of warm water and soapy bubbles.

The thing sat very still while Granny scrubbed it.

It stared around the steamy room.

It stared at Zac and Essie and Granny Mo.

Then it gave a big hiccup and muddy bubbles floated from its mouth.

Zac and Essie giggled and rushed to be first to pop them with their fingers.

"Maybe you could keep it as a pet, Granny Mo!" said Zac.

"Yes!" said Essie. "But only if it doesn't have an owner already."

"That's true," said Granny Mo. "And don't forget, it might not *be* a pet. It might be a wild animal."

The thing was all clean, but they still weren't sure what it was. Its fur was as brown as the mud it was found in. And the fur was like no fur they'd ever seen before. Instead of being hairy, it was rubbery!

"Here," said Granny Mo, lifting the thing out of the water and plopping it on the floor. "Let's get a better look at you."

The thing sat up on its back legs like a meerkat. Zac and Essie could see it had four paws altogether. Four flippy-flappy rubbery paws.

They *still* couldn't tell what sort of animal it was.

"Maybe it's too wet!" said Granny Mo, grabbing a clean fluffy towel.

The thing vanished inside the towel as Granny Mo began to rub it dry.

PLINK!

TINK!

THUD!

The noises weren't loud, but Zac and Essie heard them clearly.

Granny Mo slowly lifted the towel away and Zac and Essie saw the creature's dried fur wibble-wobble up and down. And with every wibble-wobble, something fell onto the floor.

A blue button.

A ring pull from a can.

A pink shell.

A bronze penny.

A bottle top.

A glass bead.

A purple plastic ring.

A rusty key.

A tiny doll's hand.

A dog's tag.

A yellow Lego brick.

A small silver bell.

"Isn't that a bell from your bag?" Essie asked Granny Mo.

"The thing must have come out of the mud to steal it!" said Zac.

Zac, Essie and Granny Mo stared at each other.

"Well, we don't know what animal this is," said Granny Mo, "but one thing's for sure – it's an *expert* mudlarker!"

Chapter 8

There and then GONE!

The thing sat nicely on the sofa next to Zac. The only parts of it that moved were its big eyes.

It watched Essie sitting on the living-room carpet. She was putting all the thing's tiny treasures on the coffee table one by one.

It watched Granny Mo sitting on the armchair with her laptop on her knees. She was looking at websites about exotic animals. She was *still* trying to work out what the thing was exactly.

"Found anything yet?" asked Zac as he patted the thing's head. Another flutter of bubbles popped out of its mouth.

"Nope," said Granny Mo.

Zac and Essie scooted over to help their gran. Together the three of them checked out loads of sites and heaps of weird and wonderful mammals and reptiles and all sorts. But nothing was the same as the thing.

Granny Mo gave a sigh and closed the laptop.

"Maybe we need to ring the zoo," suggested Essie. "*They'd* tell us what it is."

"Maybe we could take a photo of it and email it to the zoo!" said Zac.

"That's a good idea!" said Granny Mo, and got out her phone.

"Can *I* take the photo!" asked Zac.

"No, can I take it?" said Essie.

"*I'll* take it," said Granny Mo, turning to point her phone at the thing.

Only, the thing wasn't there any more.

"Oh!" said Granny Mo.

Zac and Essie jumped up quickly. Where had the creature gone? They suddenly heard a crash and a tinkle and the pitter-patter of rubbery paws!

Along with Granny Mo they rushed to see what the thing was up to.

In the hall they found coats and jackets pulled off the pegs and onto the floor. The thing wasn't there.

They rushed into Granny Mo's bedroom and saw feathers floating in the air from all the burst pillows. The thing wasn't there.

Next they checked in the bathroom. All the taps were gushing water, bottles were tipped over and shampoo and bubble bath were dribbling out of them. The thing wasn't there.

They sped into the kitchen and saw that the fridge, the freezer and every cupboard door was open. Pasta and rice and cornflakes spilled out like crunchy waterfalls.

"Look!" said Essie. The bread had lots of tiny bites taken out of it.

The thing wasn't there.

"Where *is* it?" asked Granny Mo.

Granny Mo and Essie hadn't seen that Zac had left the kitchen. But now he was back, with news.

"I just double-checked the living room and all the tiny treasures have gone!" he told them.

He missed out the bit about the stuffing sticking out of every cushion. And he didn't have time to tell them that the buttons on the TV remote had been nibbled off.

Then Granny Mo saw that the door to the roof terrace was open and there were no heads on any of the flowers in the pots outside.

The cousins ran out onto the terrace and looked around, followed by Granny Mo.

Zac peered over the railing. All he could see was the yard of the shop below, full of boxes and bins. But he couldn't see the thing.

"It *must* have climbed down onto the shed," said Granny Mo with a deep frown. "Is it hiding somewhere? I hope it hasn't gone in the back door of the shop!"

"No, it hasn't!" yelped Essie as she pointed to an alley that ran behind the row of shops. "It's THERE!"

The little brown creature was pitter-pattering away down the alley, holding an orange poppy in its paw.

"Where's it going?" Zac said. Worry made his words wobble.

"We'd better find out," said Granny Mo. "Hurry up!"

Chapter 9

How many monsters?

The thing was as zoomy as Cookie the cat, as tricky as Samson the snake, as nibbly as Rocky the rabbit, as messy as Chickpea the chicken and as starey as Arlo the axolotl.

But none of those pets were as interesting as the thing. Looking for it was like going on a treasure hunt!

Granny Mo, Zac and Essie ran after the thing's trail along alleys and empty back streets.

A trail of buttons, bells and bottle tops.

Twirls of pasta, dashes of rice and dots of frozen peas.

Bronze pennies, orange petals and lots and *lots* of white feathers.

The trail took them back where they started: to the stone steps that led down to the river.

"The tide's coming in," said Essie. There was only a small slither of sand bank left.

"I'm just glad it got back home safely," said Granny Mo as she bent down to pick up a shiny key from the bottom step. The key to her roof terrace door.

The three of them stared at the patch of sand bank as the river began to slosh over it.

"I wish we could have said goodbye," Zac said sadly.

"Me too," said Essie.

And then Essie had an idea. She tugged the hairband from one of her bunches and threw it hard. The round red plastic bobbles looked like a pair of cherries in the mud.

"What did you do *that* for?" asked Zac.

"Shh! Let's see what happens," said Essie.

And there it was … the mound of mud slowly rising, two googly eyes blinking.

FLOOP! A rubbery paw *snatched* the red bobbles away.

Zac and Essie saw the mound of mud vanish back into the ooze.

Only a few muddy bubbles floated back up.

"Can we come back here again *next* Saturday?" asked Zac. "Maybe we'll see it again?"

"Of course we can, my little monsters!" said Granny Mo, putting an arm around both the cousins.

"Are you sad that it didn't turn out to be a pet for you?" asked Essie.

"Oh, not at all!" said Granny Mo. "Meeting a mudlarking monster is *much* more fun than having a normal pet."

"You have us and the mudlarker – that makes *three* little monsters altogether!" said Zac.

"Oh, yes!" laughed Granny Mo. "Now, how about we go back to the flat, tidy up the mess and have some cake?"

Zac and Essie nodded.

"I'll be first to the top of the steps!" Essie suddenly called out.

"No, *I'll* be first!" said Zac.

As the cousins ran up the stone steps, they didn't see that there were some eyes watching them. Not ONE pair of googly eyes. But TWO!

Maybe next Saturday there'd be *another* little monster to meet ...